I'm Just a Kid

A SOCIAL EMOTIONAL BOOK ON SELF-REGULATION

Printed in the United States of America

Library of Congress Control Number: 2021940442

ISBN(Paperback): 978-1-7373517-0-2

ISBN(Hardcover): 978-1-7373517-1-9

Dedication

This book is dedicated to my family
and to all of the children and families that experience
BIG emotions in little bodies.
We're all connected.
You're not alone and
I love you.

All kids like to play.

Everyone knows that!

But what you may not know about me is that I

love

to play with puzzles!

Jigsaw puzzles, Rubik's cubes, crossword puzzles, 3D puzzles—for some reason, they're all easy for me

...MOST of the time.

Mom tells me I'm really smart.
She even calls me a genius sometimes.
And boy, does that make me feel like I'm

cool!

But when I'm about to finish a puzzle, and I find out I'm missing the last piece, I get so

frustrated!

Ugghh, it's not fair! Where is it?

It makes me want to

scream!

I can't help it. After all my hard work, and now I can't find one little piece?

It's nowhere!

Mom tries to calm me,

but. . . I can't. . .calm down. . .

just

like

THAT!

Maybe if I count to 100
really,
really fast
1, 2, 3, 4, 5, 6, 7, 8, 9, 10, 11, 12, 13, 14, 15, 16, 17, 18, 19

ARRGHHHHH!!!!!!

It didn't work.

"It's OK to be Upset," Mom says.

"Let's think about the things that calm you down."

Hmm....

Well, sometimes when I take a walk and come back it helps me.

It even helps me when I take three deep breaths.

Like... eating a pizza and blowing on the pizza—wait. . .no. . .

I'm supposed to *smell* the pizza, and *then* blow on the pizza! Yeah, that's it.

In...out...in...out....

I decided to get in my blanket this time.
It always makes me feel

calm.

It reminds me of a little bug in a rug!

Mom hugs me. She cries when I cry.

And then she smiles and says,

"I know it's tough. It's OK."

I am just a kid. I am smart. I am fun, and

I have big emotions. But that's me, and that's

OK.

I am in **control.**

I am **smart.**

I am **fun.**

I am **safe.**

I am **loved.**

I am **brave.**

Printed in the USA
CPSIA information can be obtained
at www.ICGtesting.com
LVHW071332011123
762330LV00019BA/251